Ghost Rescue

AND THE

GREEDY GORGONZOLAS

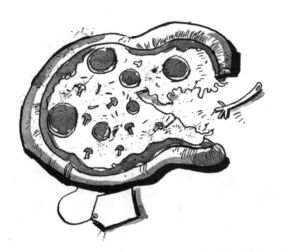

WRITTEN BY
Andrew Murray

ILLUSTRATED BY
Sarah Horne

ORCHARD BOOKS

ORCHARD BOOKS
338 Euston Road, London NW1 3BH
Orchard Books Australia
Level 17/207 Kent Street, Sydney, NSW 2000
First published in hardback in Great Britain in 2009 by Orchard Books
First published in paperback in 2009
ISBN 978 1 84616 350 0 (hardback)
ISBN 978 1 84616 359 3 (paperback)
Text © Andrew Murray 2009
Illustrations © Sarah Horne 2009
A CIP catalogue record for this book is available from the British Library.
1 3 5 7 9 10 8 6 4 2 (hardback)
1 3 5 7 9 10 8 6 4 2 (paperback)
Printed in Great Britain
Orchard Books is a division of Hachette Children's Books,
an Hachette UK company.
www.hachette.co.uk

Does anything smell as good as toast?
thought Charlie.

There it was, sticking out of the
toaster, smelling oh-so-yummy. It wasn't
Charlie's toast, it was his mum's. But
Mum was busy with baby Chloe, who had
spilled blackcurrant juice all over her
arm. So the toast sat there in the toaster,
all alone and seeming to say, "Eat me,
Charlie, I'm going cooold..."

Charlie rescued the toast from going cold – munch, munch, munch.

He was licking his lips when a voice said, "The ghost of the toast isn't happy with you, Charlie."

And Lord Fairfax appeared. In fact, Lord F had been there all along, but invisible, so as not to upset Mum, Dad or baby Chloe.

Only Charlie knew about the Fairfax ghosts. Lord F had been invisibly reading the newspaper that was on the table, wearing his invisible reading glasses.

"The ghost of the toast?" said Charlie. "What are you talking about, Lord F?"

Lord Fairfax took off his ghostly glasses and handed them to Charlie. "Here, Charlie, put these on and look at the toaster."

So Charlie put on the glasses. It felt like wearing smoke. But there, in the toaster, he saw the ghost of the toast he had just eaten.

"You stole me!" squeaked the ghost of the toast. "I belonged to your Muumm..." As it spoke, it faded away to nothing.

"Wow!" said Charlie, amazed. He felt
bad. Charlie the toast thief was also...
Charlie the toast murderer? How awful!

"Don't worry, Charlie," smiled Lord F. "Everything leaves a ghost behind – food when you eat it, water when you drink it, hair when you cut it. With the help of my glasses, you can see these ghosts. But the ghosts of things fade away quickly.

"Only the ghosts of people and animals remain."

Charlie was thinking about all of this, when there was a beep from his computer. "Ghost Rescue has email!" said Charlie with a grin, and he and Lord Fairfax hurried over to the computer.

Dear Ghost Rescue,

I need your help! My name is Lola Gorgonzola, and I have recently died and become a ghost. When I was alive I made my fortune with the Gorgonzola Pizza Company. My family are greedy and grasping, and all they want is my fortune. I don't want any of them to have it, and so I have hidden the treasure in a secret place here at Gorgonzola Mansion. But my relatives won't leave me alone! They keep summoning my spirit, and then they try to find out where I've hidden the treasure. They ask me, they bully me, they try to trick and threaten me – but I refuse to tell them! But oh, Ghost Rescue, they just won't leave me in peace. Will you help me?

Yours in hope,

Lola Gorgonzola

"Hooray!" cried Charlie. "Ghost Rescue has its first job!"

What excitement! Charlie and the ghosts – Lord and Lady Fairfax, their daughter Florence, Zanzibar the dog and Rio the parrot – got ready to visit Lola. Charlie's room was filled with chatter.

"Woof!" barked Zanzibar, tail wagging.

"Awwk!" squawked Rio, feathers fluffing.

"Poor Lola!" said Lady Fairfax.

"Poor us, you mean," said Florence. "How are we going to get to Gorgonzola Mansion?"

The ghosts were stuck because their spirits were tied to the foundation stone of Fairfax Castle, which Charlie had brought home and hidden in the garden.

"On my bike," smiled Charlie…and he went into the garden with a hammer. He returned with a piece of stone in his hand.

"Here!" he grinned. "A piece of the Fairfax Stone. Now, wherever I go, you can all come with me!"

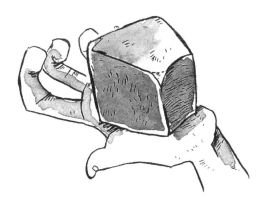

Charlie cycled through the rain, the piece of Fairfax Stone in the bag on his back and all the ghosts floating invisibly beside him.

"Phew-wee!" panted Charlie, spitting rain. "I wish Ghost Rescue had a car." But soon, through the wet, the great gates of Gorgonzola Mansion appeared.

"Oh, thank you for coming!" said Lola Gorgonzola.

"How can we stop your relatives pestering you?" asked Charlie.

"You could talk to them, Charlie," said Lola. "If they won't listen to a ghost, perhaps they'll listen to you..."

All the Gorgonzolas were there,
getting ready to summon Lola's
ghost again.

"How many more times do we have
to go through this?" growled Lola's son,
Santiago Gorgonzola, a grumpy, grey
bulldog of a man. "My miserable old
mother – how can she do this to us?
Her family?"

"I'm running out of patience, Santi,"
hissed Santiago's wife, Maria. "If your
mother doesn't tell us where the loot is
this time, there are other things we can
try. We can—"

"Excuse me?" said Charlie, tapping on the door.

"What?" said Santiago. "Who are you, boy?"

"I live nearby," said Charlie. "Lola spoke to me. She asked me to tell you to stop summoning her."

"Lola spoke to you?" snarled Santiago. "And who are you, boy, to be talking with our mother? Eh? Are you a Gorgonzola? Are you?"

"No," said Charlie. "But—"

"But nothing!" hissed Maria. "This is family business, and no business of yours. Go on, get out, go home, before we call the police!"

"No good," said Charlie. "They said—"

"We heard," sighed Lord Fairfax. "We were all there, listening."

"I didn't think it would work," said Lola sadly. "I know my family only too well. But it was worth a try."

"So what now?" asked Florence.

"Now…" said Lola thoughtfully. "Now I have another plan. But to make the plan work, we have to keep them busy for a while. Charlie, I want you to draw a treasure map, full of clues, to show my family where the loot is buried."

"Eh?" said Lord F. "But we thought–"

"It will be a fake treasure map!" smiled Lola. "Charlie, you'll find pen and paper in that drawer…"

So Charlie sat down and began to draw a map of Gorgonzola Mansion and all the surrounding gardens. The map got very messy, full of crossings out and corrections, and none of the clues seemed to make any sense.

"But that's good," smiled Charlie. "The messier it is, the better. This will really get the Gorgonzolas scratching their heads!"

So Charlie put the map in a drawer, with one corner sticking out temptingly, and Santiago and Maria's skinny, sour-faced son, Paul, found it.

"Mum! Dad! Look at this. I guess we don't need old Lola anymore!"

MARKS THE SPOT

And indeed the Gorgonzolas forgot all about summoning Lola, and now that the rain had stopped, they charged into the Mansion's muddy gardens.

Santiago insisted on holding the map,
Maria pointed and barked orders, and
Paul demanded to look at the map – after
all, he'd found it. They argued and
bickered, and with spades and shovels
from the gardener's shed they dug here,
there and everywhere, and made a
horrible mess of the lovely lawns and
flowerbeds.

Charlie, meanwhile, was starving. And since all the Gorgonzolas were outside, he decided to stroll down to the kitchen.

"Who are you?" asked the cook.

"Er...I'm Charlie Gorgonzola. Santiago's sister's cousin's brother-in-law's...er... son."

"Oh, *that* Charlie Gorgonzola," said
the cook, and she left Charlie to open the
enormous freezer.

There it was. It was wonderful. It was beautiful. It seemed to say to Charlie, "Eat me!" It was the most gigantic pizza Charlie had ever seen, or even dreamed of. It had mushrooms, and tomatoes, and anchovies, olives, ham and cheese, and Charlie could taste it already.

For a special occasion ONLY!
Lola x

There was only one problem – stuck
on it was a big label that read: *For a special
occasion ONLY! Lola x.*

"Well, I am specially hungry," reasoned Charlie, and he asked the cook to pop it in the oven.

Meanwhile, the Gorgonzolas were still fighting over the map.

"Look!" said Paul, grabbing it,
"I found this map, and I want a look—"

"Hey!" cried his father. "Watch what you're doing. Your hands are wet – you're smudging the clues."

"My hands are perfectly dry!" protested Paul. "It's the—" And he stopped, as he realised.

"It's the ink!" gasped Maria.

"It's wet!" gasped Santiago. "This map is — a — FAKE!"

Faces red with fury, shoes brown with mud, the Gorgonzolas stamped back into the Mansion.

"Draw a chalk circle!" roared Santiago.
"Cover it with magic symbols! We're
going to summon that old witch Lola
again – but this time we're going to hold
her prisoner!"

They sat in a circle, the whole Gorgonzola clan, with their lawyer, Mr Wrenchpenny, looking on. They joined hands, and recited the spells…and Lola felt her spirit being pulled, like a dog on a leash, into the magic circle. There she was trapped. The magic symbols held her as strongly as iron bars would hold you or me.

"No more games, Mother," snarled Santiago. "No more fake maps. No more tricks! We're not going to let you go until you tell us where the treasure is!"

Lola looked at them all, at their angry, hungry, greedy faces – and smiled.

"I could tell you where the treasure is, my dear Santi…" she said. "But it wouldn't do you any good."

"What do you mean?" snapped Maria.

"I mean that the treasure no longer belongs to you. I've written a new will, and all of my fortune is going somewhere else. Charlie? Will you bring in my new will?"

"Him!" spluttered Santiago. "That horrid little boy! I knew he would be trouble!"

Charlie carried a large, important-looking piece of paper in one hand and wiped bits of pizza from his mouth with the other. "Here's the will, Lola."

"Charlie wrote it out for me," smiled Lola. "I now leave all my money to…Ghost Rescue."

"You can't do that!" cried Santiago.

"A ghost can't change her will!" hissed Maria. "Mr Wrenchpenny, tell her. A ghost can't change her will!"

"Well…" said Mr Wrenchpenny, with a deep sigh. "Technically, legally, there isn't anything to stop a ghost changing her will – as long as she has two witnesses."

"Aha!" cried Santiago. "There, Mother! We've got you! You've only got one witness, that nasty kid. You're a witness short. Ha ha ha!"

"Not so!" said a commanding voice – and Lord Fairfax appeared, followed by his family. "I have also witnessed Lola's new will. It is the law – and there is nothing you can do!"

The Gorgonzolas screamed and shouted, argued and protested, bullied and threatened – but it was no good. Lola and Charlie knew it. The Fairfaxes and Mr Wrenchpenny knew it. It was the law – and there was nothing that Santiago, or Maria, or any other Gorgonzola, could do.

The Gorgonzolas drove off in a furious roar in their fancy Mercedes. Maria leaned out of the window. "Curse you!" she shrieked. "Curse you all, you filthy ghosts, and curse you, Charlie, you horrid, horrid boyyyyyy…"

Charlie sat down in the kitchen to
finish the rest of his mighty pizza. It had
turned into a celebratory meal.

"Wonderful!" he cried, with his mouth full of cheese and tomato. "Wonderful! Now all we have to do is dig up the treasure, and Ghost Rescue will have some money! So, where is the treasure, Lola?"

"Um…" said Lola. "The treasure, yes…er… Oh dear, it's slipped my mind. Let me think… Oh dear…" And the harder Lola tried to remember, the worse her memory got.

"Oh dear," echoed Charlie. "If only there was a real treasure map…"

"That's it!" cried Lola. "There is a map!
A very special treasure map – I made it
so that nobody would see it for what
it was. I disguised it. Now, what did
I disguise it as…?"

She looked around for ideas – looked
left, right, up, down – and saw Charlie's
pizza.

"THE PIZZA!"

Charlie nearly choked.

"THE PIZZA?" cried everyone but Charlie, who was having a coughing fit. And everyone looked at the pizza with fresh eyes.

"There it is!" laughed Lord F. "Why didn't we see it before?"

There it was indeed, a map of Gorgonzola Mansion and its gardens, laid down in perfect detail on the pizza. There, spelled out in little anchovy letters, were all the clues to where Lola had buried the treasure.

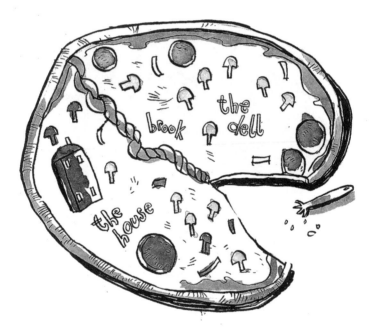

Well, not quite all the clues…because one piece of the map was missing. A big piece.

"Charlie…" said Lord F.

"That piece of pizza you ate…" said Lady F.

"That was the most important piece!" said Florence. "That was the piece that showed where the treasure is – and now it's gone, gone into your greedy tummy!"

"Oh," said Charlie. "Sorry…"

They all sat there in despair. The treasure was lost. Charlie felt terrible. He looked around at all the sad ghosts, at Lola still trying to remember, at Lady F and Florence not knowing what to do or say, at Zanzibar curled sadly under a table and Rio tucking his beak under his wing – and finally at Lord F, who had closed his eyes and was rubbing his nose as if it itched, rubbing the marks made by his reading glasses…

Charlie jumped to his feet.

"Lord Fairfax!" he shouted. "Your glasses, quick, give them to me!"

"My glasses?" Lord F said, as he fumbled in his pocket. "Why?"

"Quickly, quickly!" begged Charlie, and he put on the ghostly glasses, and looked at the pizza again. There, fading away, but still just readable, was the ghost of the pizza piece.

"There!" said Charlie triumphantly. "There's the treasure!"

Out they went, Charlie with a shovel on his shoulder, squelching through the mud, all the ghosts floating excitedly behind him. Charlie found the exact spot, and dug and dug until he was covered in muck…and there it was! Lola's fortune, in cash and gold and diamonds and rubies!

"Are you sure, Lola?" asked Lord F. "Do you really want to leave it all to Ghost Rescue?"

"I'm sure," smiled Lola. "You've saved me, and with this money I'm sure you can save many more ghosts from trials and troubles!

"I would also like Ghost Rescue to have…*this*."

And Lola showed them a delivery van with "GORGONZOLA PIZZAS" painted on the side.

"Wow!" said Charlie. "That beats a bicycle any day!" And he opened the back (phew, it smelled of garlic), and threw the treasure and his bike inside.

Then he climbed behind the steering wheel and slid down so his feet could reach the pedals…

…And with the ghosts looking out and telling him where to steer…

…Charlie drove away.

"Goodbye Lola – and thanks for the Ghostmobile!"

Ghost Rescue

WRITTEN BY
Andrew Murray

ILLUSTRATED BY
Sarah Horne

All priced at £8.99

The Ghost Rescue books are available from all good bookshops,
or can be ordered direct from the publisher:
Orchard Books, PO BOX 29, Douglas IM99 1BQ
Credit card orders please telephone 01624 836000
or fax 01624 837033 or visit our website: www.orchardbooks.co.uk
or email: bookshop@enterprise.net for details.

To order please quote title, author and ISBN
and your full name and address.
Cheques and postal orders should be made payable to 'Bookpost plc'.
Postage and packing is FREE within the UK
(overseas customers should add £1.00 per book).

Prices and availability are subject to change.